Laced

The Second Book of the PILLBILLIES Series

K.L. Randis

FOR Q. & A.
You can never be lost if you know where you've been.

Also by K.L. Randis
Spilled Milk: Based On A True Story

Pillbillies

AUTHOR'S NOTE

Thank you to the paramedics, police officers, recovering addicts, family members and friends whose invaluable input, personalities and stories are embedded in the crux of this novel.

PROLOGUE

It was wrong of Jared to test Hailey's memory after the assault but he had to know how much she remembered of his drug-filled past. If there were any parts of his life that he wished he could erase from her memory it would be any recollection of his involvement in Lacey's death, the drugs and his stints in rehab. She was the only person who ever saw the good in him, and as deceitful as it may have been, he desperately hoped that the good was all she would remember when she finally regained consciousness.

Still, he couldn't just outright ask her about the nature and extent of her memories; it felt unfair to pressure her like that. The trauma had already erased years from her early childhood and her time spent as a teenager. From the way she'd described it, it were as though entire pages of her life were simply blank.

Missing.

Jared watched her cry in frustration as different doctors interrogated and prodded her about what she could recall. It seemed that Hailey remembered Jared, but not moving to Florida. It meant she only had more recent memories of him from when she moved back to Pennsylvania, and knew little about when they dated as teenagers.

When he told her stories about how they met she took his word for truth, even telling him how much she loved him a few days after sorting through the fog saturating her memory. The sheer idea that she could speak was profound enough; her ability to remember that they were a couple and that she loved him was more than he ever could have hoped for.

"Hey beautiful," Jared said as Hailey suddenly stirred from her sleep. The doctors were sure she would be released within the next week or two and they took pride in calling her their miracle patient. She had already undergone three corrective surgeries to her face. It had been a long few months and the bills were stacked in a neat pile next to the refrigerator, their balances threatening to drain Jared of all he had. He didn't care though, and he intended on funding the most skilled plastic surgeons that money could buy.

Her lips parted weakly and she motioned for him to move closer to her. He rested his hands on the mattress, contemplating his next move. It was selfish—he realized that—but he needed to know.

"Remember when I told you my sister died in a drowning accident?" Jared asked, treading lightly.

Hailey shook her head. "I'm so sorry Jared, I can't remember her."

"I know," he whispered, caressing her hand.

He thought that maybe if she saw a picture of Lacey the memories would come flooding back. It wasn't that he wanted her to remember that he had been solely responsible for Lacey's death. In fact, the exact opposite was true. But he had to know for certain if that memory was gone. If it was, then maybe he had a real chance at starting over with her. If Hailey had no knowledge of how Lacey died, maybe

Jared would no longer feel the need to keep proving himself to her. Maybe then they could just live happily together without the ever-present shadow of his past casting over them like a dark, suffocating veil.

Jared pulled the same photo from his wallet that he had shown her at the cemetery when they visited Lacey's grave. His mom and dad were beaming at Lacey in a soft pink, cotton dress while she sat on the floor hugging a white teddy bear. Their picture perfect happiness was a distant memory.

"I wanted to show you what she looked like. I think you would have loved her," Jared said, holding the photo up while he held his breath.

Hailey nodded, mindlessly gripping the edge of the tattered photo and pulling it closer to her face. Her eyesight betrayed her at times, often resulting in nausea or migraines when she tried to focus on reading or tedious tasks.

A soft smile spread across her lips as she cooed at Lacey's innocence and beauty. "Oh Jared, she's just so perfect. What a beautiful smile she had," Hailey said.

She lingered over the iconic dress his mom would put on her when they had special occasions, touching the photograph in an attempt to remember. "I wish I could remember," she mumbled sadly as she lowered the picture to study the faces of his parents.

"It's okay baby, I'm sure—"

"OH MY GOD!" Hailey screamed, flicking the photo as if it were on fire. It hit the wall next to her bed with a THWACK and fell to the floor. "Who is that?! Who is that man!?" Hailey squealed, sitting upright in her bed and pulling at her hair.

"Who's who baby? Hailey who are you talking about?"

"The man! The man in the picture Jared! Why is that man with Lacey, who is he?"

3

Confused, Jared crossed the room and picked up the picture, staring down at it. "The *man*?"

"That man in the picture, the one standing there." Hailey's sobs were uncontrollable, the monitor next to her bed started to heighten in speed and Jared knew a nurse would be storming through the door any second. "That man is the one who *did this to me*. He's the one who attacked me, I'd know his face anywhere. Oh my God, who is he Jared? Who is that?"

Jared's mouth was sucked dry as he fought for words, "Are you sure? Hailey your memory—"

"I *know* that's the man who attacked me. You don't believe me do you? I could never forget that face! I know that's who did it, I know Jared!"

He held the photo at the edges; entranced by the two-dimensional eyes staring back at him. They were the same eyes that had judged him, belittled him and worried for him for so many years.

"It's my dad," Jared whispered, letting the picture fall to the floor as a nurse came rushing in.

CHAPTER ONE

Jared pulled the outdated flip phone from his pocket as he positioned himself in the far right corner of the hospital cafeteria. Weak coffee was all he could manage to keep down after witnessing Hailey's episode. Once the nurses had rushed in to subduc hcr hc'd snuck away from her bedside and made his way down the maze of elevators, hallways and beeping monitors to find solace within a Styrofoam cup.

Nothing made sense.

Hailey was so certain that his dad was her attacker. The thought of him pummeling her face into a masquerade of bruises and broken flesh seemed unlikely, but the look of terror as she recognized the face in the picture was undeniable. Why would his dad seek her out, was he looking to get back at him for Lacey's death? Why not come after Tina while he was with *her* instead? His supposed motives just weren't adding up.

In fact, the only thing that seemed to be adding up—at an alarming rate—were Hailey's medical bills. Her insurance proved to be useless since the majority of her facial reconstructive surgeries were considered to be cosmetic instead of medically necessary. It left Jared with a stack of bills, thicker than a loaf of bread, on their apartment countertop.

He finished picking apart the white brittle skin of the coffee cup and gathered the remnants into a pile in front of him, pushing it into a mound of pretend snow. The wall of windows to his right reminded him that the idea was not too far-fetched. Vibrant hues of orange and red drenched the leaves of the oak trees sitting outside, and within two weeks they would all be in a heap at the roots. Fall was always a bittersweet season in the Poconos of Pennsylvania. The change was breathtaking but it also meant that a winter season dragging longer than six months was about to start.

The double doors that were propped open towards the exit of the cafeteria let Jared witness a stretcher speed past the EMERGENCY ROOM signs; three nurses and a doctor hunched over the patient as they navigated through the hall.

"It's a shame us nurses can never enjoy the fall season," Hailey's nurse had mentioned to Jared a few days earlier.

"Why's that?" he asked.

"You know we have more people coming in through those emergency room doors because of car accidents in the fall than we do in the winter with all that ice and snow around?"

"Sure," Jared nodded. "I'm sure people don't realize how slippery wet leaves can be. It's like black ice if you skid on them the wrong way."

"Wet leaves?" the nurse chuckled. "I wish it were that simple. People aren't skidding on the wet leaves, they're looking at them."

Jared arched his eyebrows at the nurse. "People are crashing because they're too busy *looking* at the leaves?"

"Ridiculous right? They come from all around to look at the foliage, the *beauty* of our area," she said, her hands outstretched at her sides. "And while they're daydreaming about the creamsicle swirl of colors outside their cars...BAM." She smashed a closed fist into her opposite hand. "Not so pretty anymore when you're rushed through the E.R. with glass stuck through your forehead, huh?"

Fall was also the time Lacey had loved most. Jared would spend hours outside with her, pushing her on the tire swing in the back of his parents' property or raking an Eiffel tower of crispy leaves for her to hide in.

Jared had made a call to Flick before sitting down with his coffee to see if she could use her resources to look into his dad's whereabouts on the night of Hailey's attack. Since so much time had passed he wasn't sure she'd be able to dig anything up, but he was feeling cautiously optimistic when the vibration of his cell phone rattled the table next to him.

"Yeah?" Jared asked.

"It's been a while, so we couldn't find much on where he was that night. There were no credit card transactions or cell phone calls that we could see."

"No calls at all that day?" Jared asked. Surely he would have called his mom going to and from work, he had done it for years. He would even find the time to call from the firehouse throughout the day sometimes, depending on how hectic his day was. For there to be no calls coming or going from his cell phone seemed unusual.

"Nothing. But there's something we did find. Were your parents planning on moving?"

"Moving?" It was highly unlikely that his mom would leave the house where Lacey grew up. His dad had struggled getting her to go to the grocery store or even the mailbox in the months following her death. The thought of his mom packing up Lacey's bedroom seemed inconceivable. "No way. My mom would never leave that house," Jared asserted.

"They sold it," Flick said matter-of-factly. "Exactly one week before Hailey was attacked. Took a huge hit too, and sold under market value. They probably had to sell it fast and the buyer paid cash according to any records we could find. Other than that, we've come up with nothing."

Jared's head was spinning. They sold the house? "Are you sure?" he asked.

"Positive. Had one of my guys drive to the house. No one answered the door, shades were drawn. It looked like the property was taken care of but there was no sign of anyone actually living there. No cars or anything in the driveway, no newspapers or mail piled up anywhere. Made a call to where your mom and dad worked too, apparently they both put in their resignations around the same time the house sold. No one has heard from them since."

"This is unreal," Jared whispered, mostly to himself.

"Do you have any family in the area? They have friends or someone they'd be staying with?"

"No one. They were both only children, no other close family nearby. All they had was us," Jared said.

He flinched considering that, in reality, both of their children were dead to them. He sucked in a breath and changed the subject. "And the police still have no leads on who did this to Hailey? Besides her identifying my dad they haven't found anything new since then?"

"Nothing," Flick said. "Whoever did it was clean and quick."

"All right, thanks. Let me know if you find anything else."

"No game plan?" Flick asked. Jared could hear a hint of surprise in her voice.

"Not for now, Flick. I need to get Hailey home and find Dex. They're my main concerns. We're not even sure how my dad's involved in this, if at all. Hailey could just be confused. Let's keep looking into it, see what we can find. Keep me updated."

"Of course. I'll continue to keep all of this info between us so we can look into it privately, I know how personal this is for you," Flick responded.

"Thanks."

Jared slid the phone into his pocket, rubbing his temple and letting the swarm of information soak in. His parents had long ago made it clear that they wanted no contact with him after Lacey died, so he didn't know what would have made them move or quit their jobs. His dad was only a few short years away from retirement and his mom was perfectly content working part time where she was. Why throw it all away? Everything just seemed too sudden and calculated. Could his parents really want revenge on him by harming the only person he loved? He could see his dad acting out of emotion and anger…but his mom? She barely punished him or Lacey growing up, she couldn't possibly be responsible for maliciously mauling his girlfriend's face for retribution. Or could she?

Jared tapped a finger on the table next to the bits of Styrofoam. Lacey was dead. They were no closer to finding Hailey's attacker and his parents were MIA. While Flick never said anything about him getting back to work, the pressure of running a chaotic empire of pill pushers was beginning to swell. Local news stations were bombarded, covering a sudden surge of robberies and break-ins at pharmacies.

A cluster of emotions boiled over into his extremities and he dragged his arm across the table, throwing the bits of Styrofoam into the air where they fluttered and danced angrily to the floor.

* * *

Flick used two manicured fingers to raise the chin of the barely conscious man in front of her. His cheeks were patched with weeks of unshaven hair and the clothes he was in had long ago expired in smell and cleanliness. She didn't care though. She brought her face close to his ear, seething as she spoke.

"Seems as though we went through an awful lot of trouble to find you and keep you here, sir. How sad that you may wind up being useless to me." She pushed his face away, letting the faint ray of light from an adjoining room highlight the bruises and dried blood that bathed his eyelids.

"I don't care what I am to you," the man mumbled. "Who the hell do you think you are anyway? Keeping me here like a dog."

"That's *exactly* what you are to me at the moment," Flick hissed back. "You were supposed to be my insurance policy on Jared. Your capture was supposed to keep him in this area searching for you and keeping him in the game. I need him in the game, don't you get that?"

"I don't care what you need," the man said, spitting the remnants of a tooth to the floor. "You're a coward, using me against him like a pawn because you can't get your shit together on your own."

Flick smiled sweetly and sat down on the metal folding chair across from him, inching herself closer. She squeezed his knees together between her thighs like a vice.

His hands and ankles were bound and secured to a chair that had been cemented to the floor. He was only unbound three times a day to relieve himself. At night, the guards she had stationed at various places throughout the warehouse were instructed to lay him on the cold floor next to the chair and cuff him. His imprisonment was vital to Flick's triumph and there was no room for careless error or any chance of escape.

"I don't think you get it," Flick said, cocking her head to the side and lowering her voice to just above a whisper. "If keeping you here as a prisoner doesn't motivate Jared to fully submerge himself into the Pillbillie way of life then you will be utterly useless to me. Get it? You're expendable then. I'll have to find a much stronger insurance policy. Someone who would really—"

Flick stopped herself, letting the smile that crept over her lips haunt the man's vision a few moments before she spoke. "That's it," she said slowly, nodding her head. "Maybe I don't need you after all, old man. Maybe I need the girl instead. Hailey would certainly serve as a much better motivator than you. That was my mistake. I misjudged the relationship you had with your son. I thought he cared about you. Apparently not the way I had hoped."

The hunting knife was pulled from her side and in a seamless motion inserted into the meaty part of the man's upper thigh just above the kneecap. Blood saturated his jeans before he even had a chance to cry out in pain but the wails forced a guard to peek his head from around the corner as Flick stood up to leave, the man calling after her.

"My son will see you for the trash you are! Where is my wife? What have you done with her? You can't just leave me here forever for Christ's sake woman, what the hell is wrong with you? All of this for some drugs? You're crazy!" Jared's dad half yelled and half wept as the hunting knife stood at attention in his thigh.

"You're right," Flick responded as she paused in the doorway. "I can't keep you here forever. Just like I couldn't keep Dex here forever once we caught him. His situation was a bit more grim though. Couldn't have him floating around while we were pretending to hunt him down, right?

He was much better off dead. I mean, at least I enjoyed watching him die. My aspirations for your capture were much more fruitful but it seems as though Jared could care less about you at the moment. His only interests include that girl of his and finding a man he thinks is still alive. Sad for you, not an issue for me."

Flick placed a hand on the doorway, biting her lower lip. "I had no idea when we kidnapped you and your wife that a week later Dex was going to go AWOL and that his disappearance alone would have kept Jared in this town working for me. That was the point. Your capture has been useless to me so far. I had no idea you weren't on speaking terms with him and up until today he had no idea you were even missing. Now if you'll excuse me, I have a press conference about the drug issues our town is facing."

"What about me and my wife? Why'd you kill that other man if Jared was after him? You should have just left us out of it."

"Too risky for me. Dex knew too much to just let him slip along waiting to be caught. We'll just have to see how much your disappearance and involvement in Hailey's assault goes above Jared's head. *We* both know you beat Hailey within an inch of her life but we need Jared to be sure of that too. He needs to hunt you down, dearest daddy, with just as strong of a prey drive as he had going after Dex. And if I can't convince Jared that you should be his main target...?"

Her voice trailed off as she made her way past the guard and out of sight, her red stilettos echoing off the hollow walls and empty passages. "I'll just have to kill you and your wife myself."

CHAPTER TWO

Hysteria broke out when Dex disappeared and the production of Lace had temporarily ceased. Junkies climbed out of the woodwork that Jared had never even heard of to introduce themselves to his Pillbillies in an attempt to bribe them for the goods. People became paranoid thinking that they were hiding a secret supply of Lace somewhere or that they were downsizing their distribution methods.

Vicious rumors resonated throughout the county that Dex had been killed by an insubordinate Pillbillie and that Lace was being cut from the production line indefinitely. Others said that Dex was well and alive but had moved on to making meth. For a few weeks the mainstream customers that had padded Jared's pockets flocked to every meth head in the area searching for the same kind of experience that Lace offered.

Everyone was chasing the high, but more importantly they were in desperate need of the cocoon of bliss that enveloped their bodies as the high wore off. The miracle concoction developed by Dex had reached celebrity status. Pharmacies were being looted in search for some drug, *any* drug, that would mimic the complexity and authenticity of what Lace could do. When the search became futile, customers either started sobering up or started to dabble in meth or heroin. The hysteria eventually plateaued, but the consequence of Jared being out of commission as he doted on Hailey nearly destroyed Flick's empire.

Nearly.

As it turned out, there *was* a secret supply of Lace secured at the farmhouse that Dex had not shipped out. When Flick stumbled upon it she nearly cried tears of joy. Immediately, she had a full fleet of police escorts rush the product to the corners of the county and beyond, their lights blaring down the dirt road that lead to the farmhouse and disappearing behind a plume of dust. The supply would buy Flick about a month's worth of time before she had to seriously start cracking down on Jared's temporary leave of absence.

Jared's car trekked towards the farmhouse moments after the police cars had departed and Flick crossed one ankle over the other, leaning back on her own patrol unit.

She watched him exit his car, running a hand through his hair as a puff of cool air escaped his lips. He was handsome; she'd give him that. Under different circumstances she might have even pursued something with him. Coming home to a shadowed, desolate house night after night was not how she imagined she'd spend her early thirties. There was loneliness between her satin sheets at night and within the Waterford crystal glasses she poured her orange juice in each morning, but the perks of living a solo lifestyle were undeniably rich in their own sense. She had everything money could buy, but longed for everything it couldn't.

"How's Hailey?" Flick asked, watching the solemn expression Jared wore instantly change to that of relief.

"Finally resting at home. She's much happier and actually has an appetite, thanks for asking. What's with the Dukes of Hazard remake?" Jared asked, directing a thumb in the direction that the patrol cars had zipped off in.

"Dex was a prepared man. He kept a stash of Lace secured in a few of the containers in the lab, about a month's supply."

The genuine smile that crossed Jared's face stirred something in Flick's chest and she had to look away for a moment. "Wow that's great," he gushed. "So what's the plan now? Where do we stand with finding Dex and with the rest of his Pillbillies? Did we weed out all of his loyal followers?"

The giddy feeling retreated as Flick jumped into business. "Yeah, not many Pillbillies were disappointed in the idea of new leadership. The Pillbillies who *were* too loyal were replaced so you have a full team to work with. Dex is still out there but we're closing in on him. I have my best guys looking for him, we're even using most of the newer tracking technology that the police force has. We'll find him."

"It's just been so long…"

"Patience. He's not going anywhere, just lying below ground for a while. This life is all he knows and all of his allies are here. He'd be stupid to skip town without money or a crew. I'm sure of it."

"So what about the farmhouse? We can't exactly jump back into business here. We'd need to relocate if we wanted to keep control over the Lace, just in case Dex tries an ambush," Jared said.

"You're absolutely right. I've already relocated most of our equipment to a new warehouse off of Mineola Road. There's a warehouse not far from the new car wash in town, you know which one I'm talking about?"

"The Wash N' Go? Isn't that right in the middle of town?"

"Yes, I own it. Among other things," Flick said.

"So are we getting out of the drug business or what? Kind of risky to operate right in the middle of town."

"There's a plain sight rule I've found to be exceptionally easy to pull off."

"What's that?"

"Exactly how it sounds. We operate our business within the main town, in plain sight, and curious minds are less likely to go snooping around. Most people couldn't fathom operating a drug ring right in the crux of town so no one would be suspicious of one being there."

"For good reason," Jared pointed out. "There's also a bigger risk of someone stumbling into it by accident looking for directions or something equally as innocent."

"All the more reason to have the police as your friends, huh?" Flick said, winking. "Most people avoid parking lots that have police vehicles in them. I'll be sure to have one stationed there at all times. Since it's off of a main road, no one would think he were doing anything other than flagging down the speed demons cruising through town."

Jared shifted his weight while positioning his feet shoulder-width apart, bringing his hand to his chin. He pulled Lacey's bracelet from his pocket, the *L*-shaped charm dangling inches from Flick's face. "Is that how Dex got a hold of this then? Your police friends slip him some evidence from the police station? He had it delivered to Hailey's room after her attack. I nearly tackled the nurse who delivered it."

Flick frowned. "Unfortunately, yes. I'm sorry he dabbled in your personal life. On the bright side, I bet it's nice to have something of her's to hold on to."

Jared stroked the stubble while nodding his head and darted his emerald eyes to meet Flick's when he had thought it over. He didn't want to mention the note that Dex had left behind in the cup, warning him that there was a truth he didn't know about. Perhaps Dex never fathomed Flick introducing herself as the ringleader. As far as Jared was concerned, there were no more truths to be uncovered now that he was working with the true KingPin of the Poconos. Instead of pushing the issue he switched back to business mode. "Yeah, I can see how that would work, your plain sight rule," he finally said in agreement.

Flick inched closer to Jared taking in the smell of his aftershave, breathing in silent relief that he didn't put up too much of a fight to change to a more obvious location. She needed him to operate under her conditions while still allowing him room to think he ran the show. It was a tricky balance, especially because he was extremely intelligent on and off the field.

"We expecting company?" Jared asked, his eyes suddenly cold and staring off in the direction of the tree line at the far end of the property.

A clunker knocked it's way up the dirt road with one headlight, bounding over the potholes and ruts in a way that Flick instantly recognized. "Yeah, Larry," she said.

"What's his role in all of this anyway?" Jared asked, the layer of animosity in his voice hard to ignore. "Sent here to spy on me some more? Couldn't he get enough intel on me in jail?"

"Jared…" Flick said.

"Don't," Jared replied, shaking his head.

"Fair enough. To be honest he's one of the only people I can trust in all of this, he's worked for me a long time. I was hoping you could utilize him for whatever you needed. Having a right-hand man might not be a bad idea."

"You're kidding me."

"All joking aside you need help in this," Flick shot back.

"So what, he's an informant?"

"Exactly that. According to the payroll at the police station anyway. His skills and responsibilities go much further than that when I need them to."

"But he's not here to inform on me anymore right, he's here to work for me now?"

Flick rolled her eyes at the pitch in Jared's voice. "He's here to do what I tell him to do. And for the time being he can take orders from you too. He's a slug, just point him in the right direction and he'll do your bidding. Doesn't get any easier."

"Ohhh weee is it colder than a witch's tit out here or what?" Larry said, pulling a Carhartt sweatshirt over his head as he stepped outside of his vehicle.

Jared let an exacerbated puff of air escape his chest as Flick ignored it and smiled in Larry's direction. "Glad you could make it. Found the place okay?"

"Hell yeah, nothing to it. What's up cellie?" Larry said, smiling in Jared's direction and extending his hand.

Jared ignored it and turned to Flick instead. "So what exactly is the latest on finding Dex? You haven't mentioned much about it specifically."

Larry awkwardly pulled his hand inward and stuffed it into the front pocket of his sweatshirt. Kicking marble sized pebbles with his boot he fell quiet waiting for Flick to address the question, clearly complicit with whatever she needed to say.

"We found a campsite not far from where we were originally searching. He had left some things behind so we're sure it's him and we're close. It's only a matter of time before his debts are settled."

"And I'll be the one doing the settling, just so we're clear?"

"I wouldn't want it any other way," Flick said. "I'm actually more concerned with the legislation that just passed about controlled substances. Going to shake up our routine quite a bit."

"What's that?" Jared asked.

"They're reclassifying Hydrocodone to make it harder to get through a prescription. No more refills after thirty days, they need to see a doctor not a physicians assistant to get their script and it has to be handwritten, can't be faxed or emailed over."

"So what does that have to do with us? We mainly work with Percocet's."

"Exactly. Which means that our doctors are going to be under a lot more scrutiny with their prescription writing since the next best thing from Hydro is a Perc. There's a higher demand for Perc's now, which is great for us on the business side. Street value is way up. But the DEA is going to be rubbernecking any offices that start writing more Perc scripts now that Hydro is harder to get. Obviously this is going to directly dip into the way we handle our production."

"Ah, crap."

"Yeah. Luckily we amped up the number of offices and doctors we filter through about six months ago so it's not going to red flag anything for existing scripts..."

"...But it will be hard to grow any larger than where we are," Jared finished.

"Exactly. Unless you have any ideas?"

Jared rubbed the nape of his neck as Larry stared off into the distance. "I hate to say it but really the only way to go unnoticed is to put the same business model into play across a larger region."

"More offices?"

"Yeah, the only way we could slip under the radar is to scatter the business. Less prescriptions written per office, just more offices in general."

"Makes sense."

"I also have a feeling some pharmacists we know would be willing to deal with the increased paperwork of filing the handwritten scripts, for a price of course, but it will keep them on our side."

"That's really going to cut into profit," Flick said.

Jared nodded. "There's another way, I think." He skeptically watched Larry lick a dried smudge of ketchup from his finger. "You ready for your first job assignment?"

"Me? Oh yes sir. I'm willing and able, *that's what she said*," he snickered, laughing at his own joke.

"I need you to head to the courthouse and some of our doctor's offices. Get me a roster of at least fifty names of deceased people from this area with local last names. They're a dime a dozen and would keep suspicions low. Don't go back further than 5 years or so and make sure they're at least over the age of thirty."

"What's that for?" Flick asked.

"We need to balance out the cost of paying off the pharmacists. They need a name to have on file for the scripts but we can't dip into our profits to hire more guys with pretend aches and pains. Dead people don't feel much so we'll use their names."

Flick gave an approving nod as Jared reached into his pocket and pulled out his phone. He read the screen and flipped it shut. "We good here? Need to get home to Hailey."

"All good," Flick said. She watched him cross the lawn and waited until his tail lights were a dim firefly in the distance before turning to Larry.

CHAPTER THREE

"Isn't this crazy?" Hailey asked for the third time, flipping from one local news station to the next. "It's like the apocalypse of junkies is happening right in this town."

Coverage on the escalating robberies and break-ins at local pharmacies and doctor's offices had the community in an uproar. A mixture of hearing about the new legislation and watching a few hours of the news with Hailey validated that he needed to get things under control sooner than later.

"Sure is," Jared chimed in, watching her skip channels. "Not sure what's going on. It's a modern day pharmageddon."

"Oh please," Hailey giggled.

"No really," he said, pulling her closer, careful not to kiss the wounds on her forehead. "A huge pill is plummeting towards earth and if those Pillbillie astronauts don't dismantle it we'll all be higher than a kite come Friday anyway."

Hailey gripped her sides as Jared stood up from the couch. "Pillbillies and Pharmageddons, where do you come up with these things? Hey, where are you going mister? Not leaving me again are you?"

"No, of course not. I just figured I'd go join in on the fun in town. The pharmacies aren't going to rob themselves. You want anything? Viagra? Maybe a Subutex or a flu shot?"

"I'd like some of that mango wine you brought home earlier. That's a start."

Jared nodded, making his way into the kitchen. He poured two full glasses. "You supposed to drink this stuff with all the meds you're on anyway?"

"You supposed to question my wants and needs?" Hailey asked.

"I would never, ever question your wants and needs."

Jared placed the full glasses on the coffee table in front of them and lifted Hailey onto his lap so she was straddling him. Her hair was still damp from the shower they'd taken and he leaned forward to kiss her. Her body was familiar and he took his time trailing his hands from the backs of her thighs to the small of her back.

The dips of her waist rushed warmth between his legs. He let his fingers linger over the outline of her bra before tracing her shoulder blades, pulling her closer as he reached the back of her neck.

"Mmmm, let's not, okay?" Hailey whispered. She moved onto the couch next to him, grabbing her wine and taking a monstrous gulp as she refocused her attention to the TV.

Jared leaned forward, trying to get her to look at him but she continued to stare at the glowing screen.

"We okay?" Jared asked.

"I'm fine," Hailey said without blinking.

"Fine?"

"Yeah, fine."

Jared fumbled for the remote without taking his eyes off Hailey and once the room fell silent he tried again. "Hailey? Talk to me please."

The few bandages that were left on her face couldn't hide the few tears that drifted down her cheeks and she exhaled a breath of mango air. When she turned to him he felt guilty for even asking what could have made her upset.

"Have you seen me?" Hailey asked.

She didn't need to explain. The surgeries and damage to her face were extreme and for a while in the hospital when there was so much swelling there was no resemblance to the Hailey he once knew. Over time the careful tools of the plastic surgeons sculpted and enhanced what had once been there. There were still more surgeries to consider, thousands of dollars worth, but anything she needed he wanted to give her. Hailey was not vain; she never used to spend time worrying about her appearance. She was also at a crossroads, relearning who she was from the tiny patches of memory she had remaining from the attack while not even recognizing her own face in the mirror every day. He could see how scared she was, and he didn't know how to ease that for her.

"Yes, I see you every day, each morning. And every day I am so thankful that I get to spend one more day with you. You know this is temporary," he said, touching the bandage on her chin and moving his hand to take hers, squeezing it lightly. "*This* is forever though and I'm here until this is all over."

"I'm broken."

"You're breathtaking."

He wasn't lying. Considering the level of damage that he had first seen she really did have many of her old features back. The bone structure over her left eyebrow needed to be built upon again and there was a cheek implant the surgeon had recommended during their last visit. Other than that, she was healing perfectly and even more radiantly than Jared ever thought possible.

"You know I wouldn't care if you had your face wrapped like a mummy for the rest of our lives. I love you, Hailey. I need you to know that. Your face will heal, and I'll make sure that we fix whatever you want so that you can feel like yourself again. Whatever you need."

"I know. I don't want to sound selfish saying anything about how I look. How many people don't even survive what I did? And here I am complaining that I don't feel attractive enough to want to be with my boyfriend."

"You don't need to justify any of that to me," Jared said sternly. "You've been through more trauma than anyone I know. It's okay to want things to go back to normal. And it will, I promise we'll get there."

He wiped a tear from her cheek and considered what he was saying. He was so used to not bearing responsibility for anyone else that he almost forgot how calming it was to be needed. There was a part of him that wanted to keep her safe by leaving. The dangers of his lifestyle would ultimately boil over into his personal life; he knew that, especially if she started to regain any of her long-term memories.

He watched her sigh and tug on the cords of her white hoodie uneasily. There was a life with Hailey waiting for him that he didn't want to miss out on. Her attack, regardless of the circumstances, was the ultimate second chance. He didn't need to explain his past or his mistakes. He was a fresh slate, a charming and supportive man who was by her side every day in the hospital. There was a bank account in his name that was heavily padded from the trust fund of a deceased relative—as far as she needed to know—and his parent's supposed involvement in her attack was the only smudge on his otherwise flawless record.

There was also a part of him that desperately wondered if this was the calm before the storm. Since he was working so hard to keep his lies from foreshadowing the rest of their lives together it was possible that there would be a slipup, an unintentional lapse of character that would show Hailey that there was more to his past than he wanted her to see. When the honeymoon phase dried up he would venture onward and upward as a new version of himself.

So he hoped.

"Have they found your dad yet?" Hailey asked. "Any more police updates on that? It's so weird that they just sold their house and moved. Do you think he's still in town?" She eyed the new deadbolt on the front door.

"He's not getting to you. And I'm not sure if he's still around. He'd be stupid to hang around where the police could find him but obviously here's to hoping he *is* that dumb." Jared raised his own glass and let the refreshing rush of mango fill his belly. Hailey was under the impression that the police were handling the investigation into his dad. Technically, Jared thought smiling, they were.

"There's so many unanswered questions," Hailey said sadly. "I just wish we knew why he did this to me."

"I know it's been some time since it happened, but you're still sure it was him?"

Her tone deepened. "I would never forget something like that, Jared. It was him. I know it."

He kissed her forehead and poured the rest of his wine into her glass. "I believe you. Don't worry, they'll find him."

The TV hummed to life as Hailey clicked it back on. He watched her innocently tuck a strand of hair behind a maimed earlobe and felt his heart sink, nodding to himself.

Dex *and* his dad were now on his hit list. No more games.

CHAPTER FOUR

"You know I looked up the side effects of these pills on that Google thing they have on the internet?" Larry said, passing a tray of Lace to Jared.

"Yeah?" Jared answered, half paying attention.

"Oh yeah. This crap has more side effects than my ex-wife's chili if you know what I mean. Seizures, constipation, clay-colored stools. Hey man you ever have a clay-colored stool? Who the hell reports that to their doctor anyway."

"Can't say that I have Larry," Jared said.

"Ain't no *percs* to taking this stuff if you ask me. You get it? Cause...cause they're Percocets," Larry laughed.

"Har har."

"Aw come on man. If we're going to be working together might as well get along, say?" He picked up a tray of Lace, adorning the last row across the bottom with the signature red specks.

He's thorough, I'll give him that, Jared thought watching him work. Larry wasn't much to look at but his attention to detail was admirable. He took direction better than most runners he supervised over the years, double-checking his

26

work and taking extra precautions to make sure no product was wasted.

"Double dippin', that's what I call it," Larry said. "If you don't do it right the first time you have to start all over and use extra product just to make it look right. Doesn't make sense to not do it right the first time."

"Agreed. Hey Lar, you want to finish up that batch or do you want to start stuffing VHS tapes? I don't mind either one."

"Ah I'll do the stuffing around here, don't strain your pretty little fingers boss I got it," Larry said. He pulled a barstool next to the gleaming stainless steel countertop of their new lab, grabbing a box of VHS tapes as he sat and grunting in the process. "Got a real nice set up here, huh?"

"Yeah, pretty damn nice," Jared agreed. The lab was triple the square footage of the basement lab at the farmhouse. There was no short supply of freezers or storage containers that could easily sock away sixty or so cookie sheets worth of Lace at a time. Someone on Flick's payroll owned the warehouse and there were several guards stationed throughout the building and on the premises to ensure that they could work uninterrupted throughout the day and night if they chose.

Larry wound up taking on a bulk of the responsibility for production. Even though Jared only expected him to come in a few hours a day he often found him hunched over a spray bottle or pulling trays out of the freezer around the clock.

"So what made you turn into a snitch?" Jared asked.

Larry looked up from the cookie sheet and glared. "I'm an informant. And what does it matter? I'm here ain't I?"

"Sure, just wanted to know what would push you to join the other side of the law."

"It look like I'm on the right side of the law here?" Larry asked, pointing into his lap at a pile of VHS tapes.

Jared smirked.

"It's not what I thought I'd be doing when my high school counselor asked where I saw myself in twenty years but it sure does pay the bills. Plus it's not like I got anyone I need to care for."

"No kids? Family?"

"Nope. Have some family but they're bouncing around between jail and Texas and Lord knows what else. We don't exactly get together for Christmas dinners if you know what I mean."

"So how long have you worked for Flick?" Jared asked.

"Too long," Larry replied, almost too eagerly. The moment of silence that followed seemed uncomfortable and he tapped his boot to fill the void. "I mean don't get me wrong. I love my job, but I'd like to take my money and maybe go sit somewhere warmer. Get a hot bikini-type girl to give me drinks maybe and rub that coconut stuff on me, you know?"

Jared laughed. "Yeah, sounds like a solid start to the good life."

"What about you, any kids?" Larry asked.

"None yet," Jared said. "Lucky to have the perfect woman to make them with though. No rush, I'd like to enjoy her for a few years. I'm selfish like that."

"Nothing selfish about it."

"I don't think so either. So can I ask you something? How'd you wind up in jail like that? I know Flick has her ties but damn… she must have strings being pulled all over the place to set up a scheme like that," Jared said.

"Don't you forget it," Larry said seriously. "She's got more than strings. There are governors, politicians and magicians too."

"Magicians?"

"Sure. They make people disappear." Larry winked.

"Oh...right."

"Usually when she needs me on the inside we set up some kind of arrest that'll put me in county for a while or wherever she needs me. It helps that I'm on the payroll at the police station as an actual informant, less questions when she wants to move me around or request special favors. I hop in and out as she needs me. I haven't had to pay living costs in over seven years between her picking up the tab on my out-of-jail housing and actually being in jail so it's not so bad. She just needs to watch who's approving paperwork that particular week so she don't wind up in hot water is all."

"Not everyone's in with her?"

"Of course not. You have your straight arrows just like you have your crooked ones. Only difference is Flick knows how to spot the crooked ones pretty easy so she uses that to her advantage. Like the one Marshal that's got it out for her. He's been tailing her since she graduated the police academy, some guy named Price. Swears she's up to no good, files a complaint every now and then with the higher ups but she's smarter than that to get caught. It's all about who you know."

"Apparently," Jared said, shaking his head in admiration.

"Speaking of being higher up, you hear what people are doing to the Lace out on the street? They're snorting it."

"Huh? Why?"

"Gets em' a longer high apparently. Well that's a lie, the high part comes and goes quicker but for some reason the sedative metabolizes differently when it's shot up the blow hole," Larry said, placing an index finger on his left nostril. "You ever try it?"

"No," Jared said.

"Not even—?"

"No, not even once."

Larry whistled. "Well ain't that something then. You're a first."

Jared nodded. He was sure Larry knew all about his rehab stints and what happened to Lacey, Flick's job was to fill him in on the people he'd be working with. Taking care of Hailey over the past several weeks and months kept him grounded. It was tiring and hectic running back and forth to doctors and surgeons and it gave Jared something else to think about besides using.

The possibility of his dad's involvement in what happened to Hailey made his stomach turn and the curiosity was starting to eat at him. He wondered how loyal Larry was to Flick and if he would be tricked easily. If he could be, then maybe he would divulge information about Dex or his dad being found that Flick was maybe not mentioning.

There was only one way to find out.

"So Flick told me about Dex," Jared said, purposely keeping it vague. It was a generalized statement, meant to stir up any new information that might be harbored within the Intel Larry knew. If he knew anything at all.

"Oh? She did huh?" Larry said.

"Yeah."

Larry sorted the last of the Lace, carefully sliding each pill into the holding container in front of him. He snapped the lid closed when it was stuffed to the top and marked the side with a dry erase pen to indicate the date. "Well, hopefully they catch up to him soon, right?" he said finally, wiping his hands on his jeans and turning the barstool to face Jared. "It's a mess out there. Everyone's either hurting for Lace or dipping into meth or some other cocktail of pills they think is going to get them the same high. Dex is AWOL and you've the weight of the world on your shoulders with your girl at home. I know all about your dad too, that's some shit, but at the end of the day you need to remember that everyone in this has a place. I've got mine, just like you have yours. Flick's got me by the balls. I can't so much as sneeze before letting her know about it or I go back to jail for real. I need to watch myself if all of this falls apart at my feet, I don't have anything else."

Jared's face flushed. He hadn't meant to make Larry feel like a moron but he was clearly smart enough to know when cards were being played against him.

"I just want a simpler life than this," Larry sighed.

Jared nodded. "I think we all do."

CHAPTER FIVE

"Do you remember when I wrote this one?" Hailey asked, pushing another love note in Jared's direction. The blue lined paper was yellowed from years of hiding in the darkness of a shoebox in her closet, but the loopy handwriting served as a reminder that everything Jared had told her was true. She had fallen head over heels for him in high school. They wrote sappy love notes back and forth, all of which she had kept, and she even found a random journal here and there with doodles of hearts and their initials inside.

The pictures they uncovered in the boxes sprawled before them were the winning prize in their lazy Sunday afternoon. They sat together, sorting through the memories in front of the wood burning stove. Twice Jared had threatened to rip one or two pictures apart but Hailey insisted they keep them. She wanted to prove to their future children that their dad was not, in fact, always all that and a bag of chips.

"That's sweet," Jared said, rolling his eyes as he read his own handwriting. "Love you more than all the planets? What the hell were we learning at the time, Shakespeare?"

"Maybe I was. You were too busy skipping class apparently." Hailey held up a dated report card.

"This is true. Do you remember Mrs. Parson? The round lady with the thing?" Jared asked, pointing to his upper lip. He tried not to use the words *do you remember* when speaking to Hailey. Sometimes she did remember odds and ends, but often she didn't. When she did remember, her face would radiate with pride in winning a small victory with her mind.

"Ah yes! The thing! Didn't some kids call her *Thing?* That poor woman."

"She deserved it. I can't believe they'd hire someone to work at a school who hated children so much."

"Maybe she only hated you because I'm sure you disrupted her class on a daily basis?"

"I would never do such a thing. Besides, that's not the point."

"It's completely the point! I wouldn't have put up with your crap either," Hailey said, nudging his shoulder. In an instant she was pinned beneath him, his hand behind her head as he kissed her neck. "This is why it's taken us forever to get this place unpacked," she said, straining her neck to see all of the unpacking that still had to be done.

"I don't mind the boxes."

"I'm sure you don't, you're barely home," Hailey said. She used her elbows as a lever and sat upright, pulling a half empty box in front of her.

"I'm home," Jared said. He had been leaving her alone more than he would have liked but the mess that had evolved from his work absence was just starting to become manageable. Production was up and running again and Flick had some new leads on the whereabouts of his dad. He was frustrated that someone with so many open avenues of resources couldn't pinpoint the location of someone as simple as his dad, but if he didn't trust in Flick he couldn't trust in anyone. He couldn't utilize the mainstream police to locate the two people he needed to confront, given the circumstances.

Hailey sighed. "Sometimes. And sometimes you're gone for hours and can't even find a minute to text me back."

Jared nodded. "You're right. I can try to be better at that."

"Try?" Hailey asked, picking up another picture and studying the front of it. "Why would you need to try and keep in touch with me if that's what you wanted to do?"

"Not how I meant it," Jared said, narrowing his eyes. "You okay?"

Hailey's face had changed. She lowered a small picture from in front of her face, a round *O* where her mouth was. When she looked up her eyes could throw daggers. "When the hell were you going to tell me that Tina was pregnant?" Hailey asked.

The question stunned Jared. He hadn't thought of her in such a long time. He couldn't possibly tell Hailey about a pregnancy he knew nothing about. "She's what?" he asked.

"Were you ever going to tell me? Or was it something you wanted me to forget in my *delicate* position."

"Hailey I have no idea—"

She flung the photograph at him. It landed facedown a few inches from his left leg and he scrambled to pick it up. At first he had no idea what he was even looking at. It was a black and white photograph with random circles and lines splattered around. It wasn't until he looked at the top that he realized that he was looking at a sonogram.

Jared stared.

He had no idea that Hailey had kept a sonogram from when she was pregnant. She told him about her father making her move and how he 'took care of things' but she never mentioned that she had any pictures. He stared at the blob on the paper, tracing over the darkened sac in the middle and wondering how she managed to sneak the picture out of the office without her father seeing.

"Hailey, I'm so sorry," Jared started.

"You should be!" Hailey shot back, standing to her feet. "What kind of person hides this from their girlfriend. She was pregnant and you never told me? So you have a kid somewhere I don't know about?"

"No, Hailey that's not it."

"She called here the other day and I almost lost it thinking you were cheating on me and now I find this? What am I supposed to think Jared?"

"Wait, what? She called here? When?"

"Does it matter? Or did you want to return her call so you can talk about child support and Disney vacations." Hailey was sobbing at that point. She pulled her hair into a ponytail and when her hand skimmed a bandage that was resting on her temple she collapsed onto the floor cross-legged, burying her face in her hands. "Look at me! I have a college degree and according to these dean's list papers I was damn smart. Now I can't even remember what foods I like or how many birthdays I've celebrated. Who lives like this, Jared? Are you cheating on me? Do you want me to leave?"

"Hailey, sweetie, the baby was ours," Jared said. The sting in his eyes was brought on by anger. Seeing the picture made the situation so much more real and he hated her father for making that decision for her; for them. There had been a baby. A wiggling, breathing baby living inside of the woman he loved and it was taken from him before he even knew it existed.

"I…what?" Hailey said, suddenly sobering in her sobs.

"I'm so sorry I didn't tell you before. I didn't know if you remembered. I had no idea you kept this," Jared said, lifting the picture. "I didn't want to cause any more pain if it wasn't something you remembered. I'm sorry."

"We were having a baby Jared? When? I mean what…" Her voice trailed off as she looked around the room for the ghost baby that wasn't there. She quieted, tilting her chin to her chest and staring at her hands in a desperate attempt to remember. There was nothing but empty space and blurred faces for her to revisit though and after a few moments she looked up. "We were really going to have a baby, you and me? We lost it?"

Jared nodded. If she didn't ask specifically, he wasn't going to tell her all the gritty details. She didn't need the heartache of hating her parents again. Since her attack she had taken their support and help in stride, calling her mom every other day and even emailing her dad pictures of the new apartment.

If Jared could rekindle the relationship he had with his parents and have a clean slate to do it with he wouldn't want that opportunity to be shattered by something he couldn't remember anyway. He knew that her father and mother would never bring up the subject of the aborted baby to Hailey in the future—they were mum on the subject—so he gritted his teeth and prayed he didn't have to make her world crumble any further.

"Oh, Jared. Oh I just had no idea." She picked up the picture again and gently cradled it in her palm. "There's so much I don't remember. I can't believe I would forget this." Her voice was soft and before she began to cry again he pulled her into his lap and wrapped his arms around her shoulders.

"I can tell you anything you want to know," he offered.

"There's probably not much to say."

He clung to her like a koala until she shifted her position and knelt on the floor in front of him.

"I wasn't prepared for this," she confessed.

He touched her cheek. "I don't think anyone would be, baby. It happened a long time ago."

"Not just that. I mean everything. When the doctors told me that there was a chance I wouldn't remember parts of my life I never expected it to leave me this hollow. I wanted to believe that everything was happening for a reason or that I would miraculously get all of my memories back, you know like you see in the movies?"

He nodded.

"I have a degree that I can't even use because I don't remember learning anything. To be honest, I'm not even interested in the subject anymore. Everyone tells me how intelligent I was but lately I've been more interested in picking up a camera or a paint brush than opening a book."

"That's okay, the doctor's said that might happen. It's okay to have different interests or want to do other things."

"The problem is I don't know enough about *me* to figure out *what* to do. And I don't want to spend the rest of my life streaming movies and eating WaWa sandwiches to try and figure it out." She pulled at the skin on the sides of her face, dragging it to the bottoms of her cheeks. "I mean I can't even decide what to put on my sandwiches half the time anyway! Do I want mayo or ranch? Do I even like pickles? Not sure."

"It'll take time," Jared assured her.

She nodded, picking the edge of her nail. "Maybe that's what I need. Time." She made her way to the doorway, deserting the picture in the pile of memories that they were laughing about moments earlier. "I think I'm going to go stay with my parents for a little while. It's not you, I just need some room to breathe and figure out where my head is. Is that okay?"

A pang of distress rose in Jared's chest. He was losing her again.

"You're not losing me again," Hailey said, reading his face. "I need to do this for me. It's like I have Irish Alzheimer's. I forget what's even making me mad but damn it I have one hell of a grudge." She forced a smile.

He nodded with his eyes fixed on the carpet. "Sure baby, whatever you need, you know that. Do you want me to drive you to the airport in the morning?"

She thought about it. "I'd rather take the bus. It'll take longer to go from A to B, give me some extra time."

He moved next to her in the doorway, caressing her cheek and intently checking her eyes. The last thing he wanted was for her to leave but maybe it would give him time to straighten things out at home and figure out why Tina had called. With his dad still technically missing, maybe it was better that she left the state for a while and stayed with her parents. At least she would be out of harms way and he could focus his efforts on getting their lives back. "And you'll come back to me?" he asked.

She nodded and kissed his cheek. "As long as you'll be here waiting for me, I'll be back."

CHAPTER SIX

Two days later Jared was standing on the porch of Tina's apartment in Stroudsburg. Even though she only moved twenty minutes from their last apartment he had trouble finding it among the other identical row homes that lined Main Street. When he had helped her move her things out of their old apartment he didn't waste time noting the color or numbers on the side of the house but he did notice the same grey blackout curtains they once shared hanging in the window of one row home. He was sure he'd located the right place.

She always talked about moving to Stroudsburg when they were living together, like it would be a step up from their lifestyle in Brodheadsville. She treasured being able to walk the sidewalks, bouncing from getting a pedicure to a Starbucks coffee all within the same three blocks. Jared always hated the hodgepodge of shops and people that were so easily accessible. It certainly would have made his job easier in finding willing runners and pushers since statistically the more populated an area you lived in the better the chances were that someone would be looking to be a drug dealer, but he preferred the quiet of the internal town nestled between the mountains to kick off his shoes at night.

He banged on her front door for a third time, tapping his foot and checking his watch. If she still had her job she would have been home by then. The curtains suffocated any chance he had of peering inside so he made his way around the edge of the house to check for a back door. After navigating through a garden of beer bottles and broken plastic armchairs he rapped on the glass portion of her back door, calling out her name.

Nothing.

"Tina, I swear if you're out getting your hair done," he muttered, placing a hand over the doorknob. It turned readily and the blaring noise from the television inside alluded to why she couldn't hear him. "Hey yo, Tina!" he called out.

Still nothing.

The blackout curtains held true to their promise and he stumbled around the cluttered space in search of a light switch. "Tina, it's me Jared. You home?"

His thumb connected with a plastic piece sticking out from the wall and when he flicked it upward the disarray of garbage, furniture and used needles was paralyzing. There were two people lying on the floor next to the couch: one half-naked, the other half Chinese. Their snoring only became apparent as Jared clicked off the TV. When he noticed Tina slumped over in a corner near the front door, cell phone in hand, he ran to her.

"Tina, Tina wake up," he said, shaking her shoulders. When her head fluttered backward at the motion he gasped, dropping his hands to his sides and staggering away for just a moment. He barely recognized her face.

Craters invaded where baby smooth skin once was, littering her forehead and jawline. The absence of her sunken cheeks was noted and glancing down at her frame he wondered how someone so skinny could even be breathing. The aroma from her clothes was abominable and if it weren't for the fake heart-shaped hooped earrings dangling from her ears that he had bought her, he would have thought that it wasn't Tina at all.

"Can you hear me?" he asked, pushing her head back and opening one of her eyes with his thumb.

"Mmmm damn what's the deal?" she asked. She rubbed an eye carelessly, cursing as she smudged mascara into her eye, finally looking up to focus on the man in front of her. "Hey Romeo, you sure raced over here quick."

"Quick? You called me almost four days ago. Tina what the hell?" he asked. He opened his hands, watching her gaze check him over. "What have you been doing?"

"Specifically which drug or literally? The answer is different for each of those scenarios. Are you going to help me up or what?"

He moved her to the loveseat that was unoccupied by strange half-naked people and tried again. "What's going on here?"

"What's it look like?" she asked, lighting a cigarette. "You're no stranger to this life, I don't think you need a college degree to put this puzzle together."

"You're using meth?"

"Yeah well funny thing happens when you detox from that pretty little Lace pill as hard as I did," Tina said puffing a plume of smoke from the side of her mouth. "You literally crave everything and anything that you can get your hands on. Especially when they don't make Lace anymore and Dex decided to switch over to making meth."

"He did? Who said that? Have you seen him?" Jared was in Tina's face, badgering her. If she had seen Dex in the last few weeks he needed to know where.

"Calm down killer, I don't know where he is. I haven't seen him since that little shoot out at our old apartment, remember?"

"So why do you think he's making meth?"

She shrugged her shoulders. "It's what everyone is saying. They're also saying he's dead, he moved to Mexico and he O.D'ed on Lace…take your pick of which rumor to believe. I was desperate so if there was any chance he was making meth half as good as he made those pills I was going to try it."

Jared crouched down in front of her with his hand over his mouth. It was like staring into a crystal ball of what his life would have looked like if he didn't finally take responsibility for himself and take rehab seriously. She was a severe junkie now. There was no way she still had her job and from the looks of the apartment and her body it was only a matter of time before she was evicted or willingly jumped into prostitution to help feed her habit.

"What's the matter? Don't want to witness what you helped create?" she asked.

"I didn't do this," Jared sneered.

"Oh right, it was me who snuck out at all hours of the day and night to run an underground drug empire while my significant other slept. Give me a break. You think your role in this is innocent? Look around. I'm not the only half-empty soul lingering around this town anymore. You brought this crap into my life and now I don't know that I'll ever be able to think clearly again." She tapped the side of her temple with her eyes closed, rocking herself and inhaling a deep drag of her cigarette. "Shit it's cold in here, you see a sweater anywhere?"

Jared wasn't about to go poking around the room looking for a clean or needle-free garment so he stood up and pulled his sweatshirt up over his head. He flattened his t-shirt and turned the hoodie right side in before handing it to her.

"Yummy," she said sleepily, crushing the butt into the carpet and pulling the warmth over her head. "Smells like you."

"Why'd you call Tina?" he asked.

She shrugged her shoulders. "Who else was I supposed to call? I have no money, no food. My electric is about to be turned off and I haven't worked in weeks. The high is all I'm after anymore, I can't even sleep without thinking about it."

"You need help."

"I need you to help me. Do you have anywhere I can go? Some money maybe?"

He started to open his mouth but stopped. There was nothing he could do for her. He already knew how the scenario would play out. He used to do it himself, for too many years. She was going to go to rehab, probably once or twice. She would relapse, hit rock bottom harder than she ever thought possible and swear to never do it again. Her family would be robbed blind of their money, their time and their resources if they let her. The idea of her having any semblance of the life she had before was destroyed the moment she let Dex slip that red and white pill between her soft lips. His heart ached for her, but it also ached for himself.

And for Lacey.

And especially for Hailey.

It was sobering, staring into the face of someone he cared so much about at one point in his life and feeling nothing but disgust and regret. He saw himself in her position, begging someone who she thought still cared for money that would ultimately wind up getting shot into her veins later on that night. The cycle was depressing, dark and deadly.

"Jared, what the hell?" Tina exclaimed as Jared picked her up over his shoulder and started towards the front door.

"Tell your friends goodbye, you're going on vacation," he said. He offered her no explanation as he carried her into the brisk fall air, kicking and screaming the whole way.

"I'm not even wearing a bra!" she shouted.

"Shhh," he said, pressing his finger to his lips as he set her down in the front seat of his car. "Quiet now. You called me for help, I'm here to do that. Let me or I'll walk away and you'll never hear from me again."

She settled down and eased her breathing as he rounded the car, starting it and pulling onto Main Street. "I didn't ask to be kidnapped," she said.

"You might as well have."

"Where are we going?"

"Where do you think?"

"I can't go to your place, Jared, I don't think Hailey would appreciate that too much."

"My apartment?" he asked, looking at her for just a moment as he turned onto Interstate 80. "You're going to rehab Tina."

"The hell I am! You can't bring me there, pull this car over right now. I'm not living in some half-way home for junkies talking about my feelings."

"If you seriously wanted my help you'll do it. And stop shouting I'm sitting right next to you."

"I'm upset!"

"Good!" he yelled back.

"Jared please, I can't afford rehab there's no way I can pay for it."

"Not buying it Tina. Your parents are loaded and you know they'd pick up the tab if they needed to. If they don't then you'll find a way to make it work."

"It won't work! Rehab doesn't work Jared."

The rumble strips exploded underneath the car as Jared veered off the road and onto the shoulder, throwing the shifter into park so suddenly that Tina put her hands out in front of her to stop her face from colliding with the dash.

"It works if you want it to damn it, don't you see me?" he exploded. "You think I don't wake up every day thinking about getting high or how fun or relaxing it used to be? It's easier to bake myself into a coma or go sit on my couch melting into the day, it'll always be easier. This is the hardest thing I have ever done in my life and I have a dead sister hanging above my head constantly reminding me that I fucked up. I killed someone Tina, a baby girl is dead because of me, and I have to live with that every day. Every time I need to make a decision or take responsibility for something I want to go sit in a corner with my baggie of pills and let it all fall away but I can't. My parents have disowned me and it takes every cell of my being to not run back to that life. I'd be a millionaire if I had a penny for every single time I think about how different my life would be if I hadn't started popping pills after high school, but it doesn't matter. None of that shit matters."

Jared's rage filled the car. "What matters is that I finally woke up. I finally snapped out of the fog that kept me suffocating and running back for more and as much as I hate to say it out loud, God help me for saying it out loud, Lacey dying was the best thing that ever happened to me. I can't let her down twice, I just can't. So if you want to keep going down the road you're headed down I can tell you there's nothing but pain and death, along with the loss of every valuable relationship you will ever have in your life. I can drive you to rehab, I can sit in the classes and hold your hand through them and I can pretend that the money you ask me for isn't going towards your addiction. But at the end of the day the only person you have to answer to is yourself and if that alone doesn't crush your soul to the core and make you wake up and change something then you *never* will and your life as you knew it is over. No one can do this for you, but if I don't at least try to get you to see that then I'll have let two people I cared about die and I can't…"

Jared rammed his fists into the steering wheel as his voice trailed off. The tears were hot and heavy on his face as he pounded his frustration into every inanimate object in front of him. When he started screaming he felt arms around his shoulders and a soft voice echoing in his ear. After a few moments he leaned forward and put his head against the steering wheel in exhaustion.

"Okay Jared. Okay, you're right, you're right. What did I do? Oh what have I done to myself…" Tina sobbed.

CHAPTER SEVEN

The cemetery was barren. Lacey's headstone still had a striking sheen to it that brightened up the somber fall backdrop behind it. Everything around him was dead. The brittle leaves, the browned grass, and Lacey. In the spring two of those three things would come back to life. They would get a second chance, like he did, and hopefully amaze and flourish for another season as if they didn't remember the bitterness of the raw winter.

Lacey wouldn't be so lucky.

He laid a pink carnation at the base of the marble and knelt there for a few moments, lost in time and purpose. When he needed a better glimpse at the choices he was making he found himself in the cemetery, reminding himself of where he's come from and fighting to continue making the choices he knew would keep him sober. The struggle was just as emotional as it was physical and there was never a day that the mistrust in his own decision-making abilities burdened him with.

"I don't know what to think anymore Lace, about Dad and about Dex. Sometimes I feel like I'm chasing an imaginary bunny down the rabbit hole putting my efforts into this."

The wind whipped around the open field and against his cheeks. If he had been crying the tears would have surely froze.

"It just doesn't make sense with Dad, you know? I mean I knew he was angry about what happened…what I did to you. I just can't see him hurting someone like that, can you? He wouldn't hurt Hailey, would he?"

The sun was failing at trying to peek out from behind the soggy clouds overhead. Jared wasn't sure why he talked to Lacey like she would respond but it made the connection to her real. It kept her alive, in a sense, to talk to her out loud instead of just remembering her picture in his head.

He tried to remember the last time his whole family was together and actually enjoyed each other's company. Lacey had celebrated a birthday not long before the accident and she had wanted to go to the Philadelphia Zoo. Jared tagged along, watching her zip down the path in front of them, smiling behind her as she called out the names of the animals she saw. His mom and dad held hands, calling out to Lacey when she toddled too far ahead or when she threatened to put some type of foreign object in her mouth.

They ate at the Zoo's café and Lacey made Jared wear a zebra bib as he ate his cheeseburger. After they left and when Lacey started to complain that her feet hurt from all the walking, he had lifted her above his shoulders and nestled her legs on either side of his neck. She would bend over his head every few minutes, hysterically laughing and giving Jared what she called, from her newfound height, 'giraffe kisses.'

His mom panicked when she realized that it was beginning to get dark and that they genuinely had no idea in which direction the nearest exit was. She was always a worrier, a hot mess with directions, but sweeter than raspberries.

His dad sauntered over to the refrigerator-sized billboard that depicted a map of the park and stuck his thumbs in the belt loops of his jeans. He leaned forward, squinting at the maze of paths and colored icons, rubbing the stubble on his chin. "You can never be lost if you know where you've been," he had said. Sure enough, within a few short turns he had navigated the family toward the exit. Lacey clutched a white balloon in her left hand, sleepily blowing kisses to Jared as she swayed on her mom's shoulder.

Jared realized he was smiling as a whip of arctic air flung him back to the loneliness of the cemetery, his dad's words echoing in his head. "You can never be lost if you know where you've been," he whispered to himself.

The weight of the words sunk in and he looked up at Lacey's headstone. Jolted by the overwhelming ignorance surrounding his father's disappearance, Jared scrambled to his feet and raced towards his car, calling out over his shoulder, "Lace, I know where Dad is!"

"How could I have been so *stupid*," Jared yelled at the windshield, as he tore down the dirt road of the cemetery towards his apartment.

His dad lost a piece of himself shortly after witnessing the traumatic attacks of 9/11. As a NYC firefighter, he spent countless months in the aftermath of the World Trade Center attacks searching the rubble and debris for his fallen brothers.

If a body part or badge was ever identified, he had to notify the family, holding their hysterical wives in his arms. There were times that nothing was found and the pain of never knowing where their loved ones took their last breaths tore into the core of the families he had to report empty knowledge to.

Jared's mom was a worrier. She always was. Her worrying only escalated as his dad relayed stories to her when he would be able to make it home. So when his mom caught wind of a new piece of technology—tiny little stickers that you could place on anything, like a purse or remote control—where you could track it's location with your smart phone, she raced out that afternoon and bought it.

When his dad got home after a long week of digging through the wreckage of Ground Zero, his mom pulled out his dad's wallet and his cell phone and stuck a tile on the inside of the leather. The tiles only had a one hundred foot radius in order to be able to ping a location on the cell phone, but the idea was that his dad always had both his cell phone and his wallet on him at all times so they'd both be within the parameters.

She even stuck a tile on the inner fireproofed seam of his work gear. She downloaded the app to his phone and to a spare phone she kept in the junk drawer as a back-up. Even if somewhere down the road he managed to leave somewhere without his cell phone or wallet, the app would save the last known location. She religiously replaced the tiles every year, as updated versions came out, and it gave her the peace of mind she needed to kiss him goodbye every morning. Knowing that she could open the junk drawer at home and see where he was located at any time saved her sanity.

His mom was a fucking genius.

Jared pushed through the front door of his apartment and headed into the spare room. He located a box marked OFFICE STUFF and dumped it's contents on the floor. The cardboard box hit the adjacent wall as Jared fell to his knees skimming the clutter. He grabbed the familiar black-shelled phone and held the power button.

As it booted up he recalled the day his mom realized that he had stolen the cell phone from the junk drawer. The promise of an extra hundred bucks was all he needed to swipe it when he was low on cash and he spent the next week convincing his mom that she must have misplaced it and she would just need to go buy another spare phone to track his dad.

When a pusher came through with scoring a large client on the outside of Scranton hours prior to him selling the phone at GameStop, he had thrown the phone in the back of his dresser, completely forgetting about it and too proud to put it back in it's right place to prove his mom right.

He was so glad she was right.

The thudding in Jared's chest was immeasurable as the phone kicked to life and he swiped the home screen. Within two seconds he spotted the app and tapped the corner of the screen. A blue wheel dramatically spun as a message of 'Please wait while we load the last known location' flashed underneath it.

The chime that told Jared that the location of the tile had been found was deafening. "Hell yeah!" he yelled, swiping on the screen to bring up the map.

He pushed his two fingers apart, zooming in on the glass and brining the street names into focus. As he squinted, much like his dad did at the zoo that day, he mouthed the name of the streets and his own voice caught in his chest when he recognized the location.

Mineola Road, right in Brodheadsville. Specifically, right where the Wash N' Go car wash should have been. The car wash Flick owned.

"Right in plain sight," Jared whispered, repeating Flick's concept. He stuffed the phone into his pocket and headed towards the front door.

CHAPTER EIGHT

Jared turned off his headlights as he approached the Wash N' Go, innocently cruising into one of the self-serve wash stalls as though he were a paying customer. The seasonal time change from the week prior would give him plenty of cover as night fall blanketed all around him, but he knew Flick would have his men carefully watching wherever his dad was being held.

The icon on the smartphone pulsed as it glowed a downward arrow towards the part of the property where it was picking up a signal. Jared had never noticed any other structures on the plot whenever he drove by the car wash so it meant he would need to do some searching by foot. He locked the car doors and stuck his keys under a wheel well just in case he was found and frisked. He needed a quick getaway, he just wasn't sure from what or who.

The thicket that lined the edge of the property was compact. Jared pulled a hunting knife from his left side, slashing in front of him, stopping every few feet to listen but only hearing the passing cars on the main road.

He was going to kill his dad when he found him. He had already decided that on his way over. If Flick had him hostage in one of her warehouses it meant that she had finally found him and was likely planning on calling Jared in the morning.

His dad had no excuse. It was Hailey's pain from her attack that forced her to leave him. It was her recovery that he struggled to watch her try and overcome and it was his father's hands that had depleted the life in her eyes when she told him she needed time.

All Jared had was time.

Time would ease the pain of Lacey's death and the weight of his own mistakes. Time healed his addicted mentality, showing him over and over the inevitable impact of a little white pill with red specks. Time gave him a life with Hailey, and time also took that away.

His dad was out of time.

The warehouse hanger seemingly came out of nowhere as Jared pushed through the last of the brush and knelt down on the cold earth. His breath danced around him as he surveyed the darkened mass and double-checked his phone to make sure he was on target. A matured Wash N' Go sign was tilted on it's side holding up one portion of the outside wall. From his observations it looked like an abandoned building that maybe held old car wash cleaning supplies or possibly was even a futile rendition, at one point, of a space to be transformed into a larger indoor car wash arena.

There was one dove-colored unmarked police car tucked close to the tree line on one side of the building. Since it was a weekday Jared hoped that the manpower would be minimal on site. One or two guys max. He would need to create a diversion to have them come outside so he could weasel his way inside.

As if on cue, an obscure outline of a man appeared by one of the doorways. A heavy fog of smoke drifted over his head and Jared smiled.

Cigarette break.

Working fast he inched his way back through the trees and slivered onward until he was still within eyesight of the front door but far enough away that it would give him time. He knew confronting Flick's guys would only complicate things. He needed to lure them out.

He used his back as a shield as he worked, gathering dry leaves and twigs around him. He didn't want to watch the whole place go up in flames so when he was sure the perimeter around his leaf pile was efficiently cleared he lit the lump into a blaze with the lighter that was still hostage in his pocket from meeting Tina.

There were only a few seconds before the pile would give off enough light to expose Jared's presence. Once he was convinced that the fire would catch, he bolted in the opposite direction, careful to keep his shadows from dancing with the light.

The guard's back was facing the fire as Jared settled into a spot not far from the doorway where he stood. He puffed on the end of his cigarette, shifting from one foot to another and glancing, every now and then, upward at the night sky.

"Come on you moron, look behind you," Jared pleaded.

The guard hacked into his sleeve and flicked the butt onto the concrete. Jared's pulse rose as he realized he wouldn't see the fire if he walked inside without turning around. As if on cue, a disgruntled driver blared on his horn from the main road and the guard shifted his gaze as he reached for the handle. Doing a slight double-take, he squinted into the darkness. Panic struck him as he realized what he saw and he opened the swinging door, his voice booming to alert the other guard.

"Pat! Yo Pat get out here man there's a fire. You throw a cigarette in the woods you shithead?"

A few moments later Jared heard the clunk of boots against the concrete. "What are you talking about? I don't smoke as often as you, it was probably one of yours."

"I don't smoke out there," the first guard said, motioning towards the glow of the woods.

"Ah the whole place will go up if we don't put it out. Find a bucket, something."

The door slammed behind them as one guard made his way towards the amber light show and the other went in search of a bucket. When Jared was sure they were out of earshot he rushed the door and pulled it open, just as quickly pulling it closed behind him and holding his breath as he waited to see if he was spotted.

He wasn't.

There was only a sliver of light to illuminate the space around him. He could hear water dripping to one side and a bellowing echo of nothingness in the shadows ahead. Leaving the hanger would be easier than getting in, there were plenty of other exits he could sneak through now that he knew where the guards were stationed. After taking note of several potential getaway points he moved through the corridors of the warehouse. The smell of bleach stung his nose so he was sure that the building had been used to store cleaning supplies.

He moved toward the only glowing light towards the back of the hanger. No footsteps or talking could be heard, but instead of comforting him it made him more anxious. His sneakers padded his movements and he skimmed the walls as he moved, careful to maneuver slow and steady.

The cold molding of the doorway met his back as he hesitated before advancing into the barely lit room. There was a chance there were more guards, or even Flick, standing post inside. He wouldn't be able to explain why he was there other than telling her about the tiles that he used to track his dad's wallet. He didn't care.

Turning the corner with his Glock raised he poised in the doorway, his legs framed and ready. Adrenaline helped him focus on the room and when his dad's face slowly rose it took most of his impulse control not to run over to him.

"Oh what in the…" Jared started.

The bruising around his eyes was saturated to a shade of purple Jared had never seen before. Dried blood caked his lips, eyelids and jawbone. A skeleton of a man he once knew was hunched over in a metal folding chair and a yellow janitor's bucket next to it. His hands and feet were secured and it appeared as though it took most of his efforts to keep his head in an upright position. The burly, masculine man he remembered was gone and the replacement figure in front of him was despondent and beaten.

"Jared?" Mike said, grunting to strain his eyes in an attempt to identify the man that had a gun pointed at him.

"Dad…what the hell is going on?"

"Jared, let me loose me, please help me," he begged.

Jared cleared his throat, trying to juggle the storm of emotions in his throat. "Why, so you can beat me within an inch of my life too?"

Mike shook his head, lowering his chin to his chest. The subtle rocking of his shoulders told Jared that he was crying and for an awkward moment Jared lowered his gun. "What did you do to Hailey? Was that some kind of punishment? You know you ruined her life, she can't remember anything. You nearly killed her."

"The girl? I didn't know you knew her. I had no idea who she was," Mike sobbed.

"You get kicks out of beating up beautiful women? Where's mom?" Jared asked, suddenly noticing she wasn't in the room.

"I don't know where she is son. Believe me, please. I had no idea who that girl was. They took your mother. I don't know where they have her."

"Who took her?"

"These men, I don't know. The woman was there, the one with the heels."

Jared stiffened. "What woman?"

"Flicker? Or Fern? They only said her name once so I'm not sure. She runs the show around here though. The guys are terrified of her. Do you know who she is?"

"How long have you been here?"

Mike shook his head. "I have no idea Jared, the days just blur. The only time they let me up is to use that bucket." He nodded towards the makeshift commode next to him. "Please tell me what's going on. They took me and your mother in the middle of the night, blindfolded. They told us to grab our coats and that woman separated us, put your mom in a different car and we drove for hours. I wound up here but I can only gather pieces of why. They kept calling me an insurance policy to keep you in the area. Did you know some guy named Dex?"

Jared was impressed that Flick would use a tactic like driving around in the car for a long time to stimulate that they were holding him hostage in a desolate location. When he heard his dad say Dex's name he crossed the room and in a rush of callous instinct he propped the gun under his dad's chin, seething as he spoke. "Where is that scumbag and how do you know his name? Where is he!"

"He's dead Jared. He's dead! Whoever he is Fern killed him."

"Flick?" Jared asked.

"Is that her name? Then yes, Flick. She said she didn't plan on Dex leaving and you hunting him down so she killed him because he was a liability, does that make sense? None of this makes sense to me. Please get me out of here before she comes back."

"You sold your house, quit your jobs! How do you think that makes you look."

"That crazy bitch sold our house?" Mike said, letting a gasp of air stifle under his moans of despair. "My God is that what she made me sign? All those papers she forced me to sign…"

"It's like you don't even exist. You nearly killed my girlfriend, left her for dead and disappeared."

"She was your girlfriend? Oh Jared. Oh God help me," he whispered.

Jared knelt on the floor in front of his father. The weight of the situation unfolding was unbearably complex. Layer by layer the reality of who was really governing the outcome of Jared's revenge was peeled away.

If his dad was telling the truth then Jared's vain attempt to bring Lacey's killer to justice was hijacked. Jared let his emotions and cloudiness surrounding Lacey hinder his ability to see past Flick for who she was.

In the end, Lacey wasn't the only victim. His parents were innocent bystanders to a sophisticated web of lies spun by the one person he should have been able to trust. Only the feeble leaders she originally chose to run her empire undermined her greed and thirst for power among the KingPins of the Poconos. Jared was her meal ticket back into the game and she needed him around as long as possible. When her heels were buried deep within the systems he was helping her set in motion, he was sure now that she would have had him killed too.

"You really had no idea?" Jared asked. His anger was once again shifted and displaced. "She killed Dex, you know for sure?"

Mike squeezed his eyes shut, nodding and motioning towards the side of the room. "I watched her do it Jared. He was begging for his life, talking about how loyal he was and how he didn't mean to set you off. When he realized she was going to kill him he looked at me and told me that my son would never get his revenge. He smiled at me. You wanted to kill that man yourself?"

"Something like that," Jared muttered.

Mike sighed. "I knew you were an addict but I never realized you could take another person's life."

"Wouldn't be the first time," Jared replied sourly, thinking of Lacey. "And who are you to judge? Just because you've lived the mighty high sober life all this time it makes you better than me? I can't make mistakes? What makes you so much better than me anyway, huh? Nothing."

"You're right," Mike said eagerly. "I'm no better than you in the mistakes I've made in my life."

Jared looked at him.

Mike continued. "But what makes me better than you is that I learned from those mistakes. I saw the damage I was doing to my own life and to your mother's and I got help."

Jared raised his eyebrows, not understanding the context.

"You think you're the only one who had a substance abuse problem? Ah shit. I wish we didn't have to do this here," Mike said shifting in his chair. After a lengthy gush of air from his chest he looked at Jared. "I was an alcoholic, Jared. Big time. Wild Turkey was my poison, but really any liquor."

Jared's mouth dropped. "For how long?"

"Until you were three. I hit your mom one night, sent her flying into the living room wall and couldn't remember a damn thing the next morning. She had you sitting on her hip with a suitcase in one hand when I came to. She told me that if I didn't get in the car with her that moment and go to rehab I would never see you two again. I believed her."

"So she made you to go to rehab?"

"No," Mike said. "You did." His eyes moistened and he looked away momentarily. "You were three. You'd have no daddy. Everything I ever talked about for so many years, all the dreams I had with your mom about taking you to ball games and school dances was slipping away. I couldn't lose you." Mike opened his hand inviting Jared to take it.

He hesitated at first but then reached for him, feeling the warmth of his father's hands surrounding his own in a gesture of affection he hadn't felt in years. "But I lost you anyway, didn't I, to the drugs? They took you from me anyway even though I tried everything I could to stop it. I wasn't hard on you because I didn't understand, Jared. I was hard on you because your mom was hard on me and it was the best thing she's ever done for me. Please know that."

Jared knew better than to break down there, as much as he wanted to. Launching into a boundless protective mode he shook his head in understanding and scanned the room for his dad's belongings. He spotted his dad's jacket in the corner of the room and noted that his wallet was likely zipped inside one of the internal chest pockets.

"Thanks, Dad, but I can't let you go." Jared stood up, brushing the grime from his jeans and shaking off his hands.

"Wh-What? Jared I don't understand…"

"I can't let you go, I'm sorry."

"Jared, no, please…"

LACED

"I think I know where Mom is," Jared started. "And if I'm going to stay ahead of Flick I need to leave you here so she doesn't suspect I know anything."

The color returned to Mike's face as Jared crossed his arms in front of his chest, staring at the floor and nodding to himself as he formulated his thoughts. "I have an idea."

Mike slowly nodded. "I'll do whatever I can. What'd you have in mind?"

CHAPTER NINE

The closer Jared got to the old apartment he shared with Tina the more confident he was that his mom was being held hostage inside. Flick's adage of keeping things within plain sight apparently played a bigger role in her control games than she led Jared to believe. It only took Jared and his dad a solid nine minutes to devise a way to get him and his mom safely out of harms way but the particulars would be difficult to pull off without Hailey's help.

Pulling onto his old street he pressed the call button under the favorites on his phone. HAILEY flashed across his screen and he made a face at the glowing words when he heard her voicemail right away.

He tried it again, faced with the same sweet singsong of words from Hailey's voicemail. Leaving a short message he rubbed the front of his nose and closed his phone. He didn't want to call her parent's house if he could help it but if she didn't get back to him he would need to. For now he needed to make sure his hunches were right.

Parking a measurable distance away he cut the engine and scouted the property. The once illuminated apartment was utterly dreary. It looked deserted in terms of current tenants and dark curtains blanketed the interior. If he was lucky enough that the real estate broker didn't change the locks between rentals, he knew there was still a hidden key somewhere on the side of the house he could use to get inside.

The knob turned easily and Jared pulled up on the door to prevent it from squeaking open like he used to do when sneaking inside. He had his Glock poised as he turned the knob to secure the door behind him. The living room and kitchen were exposed and empty, showing no sign of tenants. A barely visible glow under the bedroom door told Jared that he wasn't alone and he tiptoed his way to the corner of the room.

He didn't see any cars lining the street or parked out front so he had to risk opening the door to one of Flick's guards. If his mom was inside though, and mirrored the condition his dad was in, he didn't care about some bloodshed.

Placing his hand on the knob he calculated his entrance and with a rush he pushed on the door, flinging it vigorously into the wall.

He was prepared for the muffled cries and tears of his mom screeching beneath her mask of duct tape as she rocked in her chair, surprised to see him. He was even prepared for the brute force of a guard or two if they had rushed at him or pulled their guns but they never came. What he wasn't prepared for was seeing Hailey equally bound and tied in a separate chair, her head hunched over and her face streaked with just as much runny mascara as his mom. When he was sure that the room was empty he ran to her, pulling the tape from her face and letting her scream in waves of relief and panic.

"Jared! Please untie us, please get us out of here!"

"How'd you get here baby, what'd she do to you?"

"I never made it to the bus stop. They grabbed me. Who are they? How did you find us?

Jared reached to his right and pulled the tape from his mom's mouth, absorbing the bout of cries and desperate pleas from her as well. "Jared! Oh, your dad, I don't know where your dad is. I've been here for so long. The man and lady who check on us will be back shortly, you don't have much time. Get us untied!"

"I can't do that mom."

"Damn it Jared, put your family issues aside for a minute and untie us!" Hailey screeched.

All at once the room exploded in a flurry of panicked cries and yelling, both women on the verge of a nervous breakdown. While he understood, he only had moments to spare and he needed them to listen. He hated to do it, but he reached across and replaced the duct tape gags. Hailey's eyes widened to the circumference of a teacup and his mom looked like she would faint.

"I need you two to focus for a minute," Jared said, waiting for the panic to subside. When they continued to wriggle under their restraints he slammed the bedroom door shut and shouted. "ENOUGH! LISTEN!"

Both women plummeted into silence. "Dad is safe, first of all," he said looking at his mom. "I need you two to trust me. If I untie you it'll only put you in more danger. The woman who took you will know I was here and she'll kill you both. I need to think a minute. If you'll be quiet I'll take the tape off, okay?"

Nods came from both sides of the room. He removed the tape and tapped his foot, staring at the back wall and wondering how he was going to maneuver Flick into his grasp now that Hailey's help was out of the question.

"Does Flick ever come here. Er, a woman. Usually wearing heels?" Jared asked his mom.

"Yeah, I've seen her. She only comes into the bedroom every now and then though, not every time. She was here earlier with two men. She used the bathroom, mentioned something about going to some store and they left. I don't think they'll be gone long."

Jared nodded. "Hailey are you hurt, baby?"

"I don't know what's happening Jared. Did I do something wrong to deserve this? I can't remember…"

He realized that Hailey's fears were probably more outstanding than his mom's since her memory loss couldn't even help her deduct why she was kidnapped. He knelt at her side, wrapping his arms around her shoulders and letting her bury her face in his shoulder. "No baby, you've done nothing wrong. I'm here. I'll make sure nothing happens to you."

He tucked a strand of hair behind her ear and made his way into the main bathroom, scanning the room for any signs that Flick was there.

When he found what he needed he re-entered the bedroom and asked if they were ready to have the tape on their mouths secured again.

"Where are you going?" Hailey asked.

"To make sure Flick doesn't hurt anyone else anymore."

He kissed her cheeks and stroked the top of her head. Then he moved to his mom and made sure her gag was back in place. "I love you, Mom." He kissed her forehead and without another word he left the apartment and made his way to the U.S. Marshal's office.

CHAPTER TEN

U.S. Marshal Marvin Price tapped his pen against his desk wondering if he should believe the disheveled man sitting across from him. For years he had closely monitored Flick, tracing her every move and judgment call, trying to pin any of the outstanding shady business he knew she was conducting to the wall. He always fell flat and she was always just out of arm's reach. Now a self-proclaimed KingPin of the Poconos was sitting in his office, begging him to trust his story about a scandal so expansive it could promote him right into the white house. Not that he wanted that.

"That's some story, kid. You have to work with me here," Price said. "You walk into my office after calling our tip line saying that you have a wealth of knowledge about the source of this Lace pill that's been floating around the county. You spin a web of stories so twisted and deep about a law enforcement officer and some of her co-workers that I'll probably have a hard time sleeping tonight, and you want me to believe that you are just willingly walking in here to hand this gift of Intel to me because…?"

"I don't expect you to believe anything," Jared started. "All I know is that my family is in danger. I know from a fairly reliable source that your finger has been itching to scratch Flick off the radar for some time now and I thought a friendly chat about the source of this info wouldn't fall on deaf ears if I spoke to you directly, sir."

Price pressed his hands together and brought them to his mouth, subtly rubbing his mustache. After a moment he opened his hands, smiling. "So?"

"So what?"

"So what's in it for you? I can't imagine you'd want to drop all of this in my lap without some sort of deal."

"Of course not."

Price raised his eyebrows, waiting.

"I'd like full immunity for myself and my family's involvement," Jared said. After a moment's pause he added, "And a friend."

"There's always a friend," Price said. "So let me get this straight. You spill your guts to me, we take Flick down while you testify and we spin you, your family and a friend into witness protection as restitution?"

"No," Jared said leaning back in his chair. "No testifying, no written statements."

"I'm not sure you know how this works, son."

"I'm not sure you understand what kind of info I'm offering here," Jared said, cutting him off. "We're not talking about popping a dealer in a parking lot for a baggie of pills and some chronic. The magnitude of what I have will bring down an entire empire that supplies one of the fastest expanding drugs through this entire county, in addition to handing you your woman." Jared pushed a pointer finger into the top of Price's desk.

"And how exactly do you expect me to prosecute any of this without any witnesses or statement? You say you know so much yet have no idea the risk I'd be taking just taking your word for it."

Jared produced a gallon-sized Ziploc bag from the depths of his hoodie and slammed it onto the Marshal's desk. It was filled to the brim with Lace, freshly iced. The Marshal's eyes widened and he pushed his chair back. "Do you have any idea how long I can put you away for bringing that in here?" Price stammered.

"Not nearly as long as Flick will get put away when I tell you exactly where her production warehouse is," Jared said. "Her prints would be all over the place, you could nail her ass to the wall until she's over a hundred. You'll also have a chance to hear her confess to the kidnapping and murder of several people if you wire me and follow me to a location where two of my family members are, at this exact moment, being held captive."

"What kind of guarantee can you give me that her prints would be at a crime scene?"

"Not prints, blood."

"Blood?"

"Women bleed, Marshal. Once every month for one to five days as a matter of fact. You'll have your DNA evidence tying her there when you take a peek in the garbage can." Jared winked.

Price grimaced. "That all you have?"

"Of course not. At a separate location, also where a family member of mine is being held, you'll find a multimillion-dollar stash of Lace. It's a car wash actually. Equally as impressive will be the stash that is at the location where the two women are. It will undoubtedly tie Flick to each of three locations, without a shadow of a doubt that she frequented them, ran them and used them for her own power and gain."

Jared sat back in his recliner, rubbing the soft leather beneath his fingers and letting the silence help the Marshal make his decision. "So do we have a deal? No testifying, no identifying any involvement on my part at all. My family's either. I'm sure there are strings you can pull to make this all happen. Witness protection isn't our thing. We'd like to stay in the area and the only way we can safely do that is if it looks like a drug raid that was founded by the long arm of the law."

"And how do I know that you're not the one pioneering all of this?" Price asked. "You're making it awfully easy for me to swoop in and throw the book at Flick, but how do I know your involvement in this is nil?"

"I think the better question is do you really care?" Jared said, standing to his feet. "I've been pointing my fingers in everyone else's direction but my own for too long Marshal. If I have any chance in living the kind of life I want to I need this to happen. Off the record? I'm not innocent in this but there are bigger fish to fry. I want my life back. A real one. I might not deserve it but my family does. I'd like to give that to them."

"So why send you in there at all with a wire? Why not give us the locations and let us do our jobs?"

"I need to see her face when you show up. I think you can appreciate that."

"And you're sure this is how you want things to go? You seem lost kid."

"You can never be lost if you know where you've been."

The Marshal nodded. "So who's this friend?"

"Friend?"

"The one you want immunity for."

"Oh," Jared said, his teeth reaching the corners of his mouth. "You'll find him at the production house. His name's Larry. Go easy on him though, he'll probably put up a fight until he realizes he's a free man."

CHAPTER ELEVEN

It took longer than Jared had anticipated but Flick arrived at the apartment several hours after he had settled into the bedroom with his mom and Hailey. The wire seemed to weigh a ton sitting under his shirt and he had tested it several times prior to the raid. When the doorknob turned he was standing between each of the women, both of them securely tied to their respective chairs and shaking beneath their restraints. He hated to put them in the middle of the take down but he had no choice. It was the only way out.

"Jared?" Flick's face showed more surprise than her voice. On instinct the guard raised his Glock but Jared remained poised and calm. "Put that down Greg, he's with us." The uneasiness of her voice in her statement was validating. She wasn't sure what side Jared was on at the moment, he knew that, and she darted her eyes from his mom to Hailey then back to his. "What's going on here?"

"I needed to give you this," Jared said. The cell phone cruised through the air and in reflex Flick opened her hands to catch it.

She looked down at the phone, not understanding. "What for?"

Jared shrugged his shoulders. "You know you underestimated me, Flick. I had no doubt you would find Dex eventually, but I was sorry to hear that you had killed him. I'm not sure that was part of the plan."

Flick cocked her head to the side. She couldn't understand how Jared had found his mother and Hailey or what he planned to do. She didn't have the patience or time to wait it out either. "I did what I had to do given the circumstances. He was no use to me alive."

"How's that?"

"He knew too much. Particularly, he knew too many ways in which I could eliminate you if and when the time came and that was too much of a liability to me."

"And I'm not now?"

"I think you know the answer to that. I also think we both know you won't be leaving this room alive or with your family as you probably hoped. I have two men waiting at the door and another in the car. Perhaps you underestimated me, Jared. I'm not sure why you felt the need to snoop around." Flick eyed Hailey, a shadow of disappointment clouding her eyes. "For a moment I cared about your motives when I first opened this door but in all reality, you've set the train in motion and I don't believe I'll be needing you any longer. This is where you jump off."

She raised her own Glock, positioning it at a parallel with his head. Hailey started to rock back and forth in defiance. "Keep rocking and I'll kill you first, girlie," Flick said, her eyes never leaving Jared's. "I'm disappointed Jared. I thought we were on the same page with things."

"Oh, like this page?" Jared asked, opening the bedroom closet. A tumbleweed of gallon-sized Ziploc bags tumbled onto the floor. A few million dollars worth of Lace was sprawled on the floor in front of them and stuffed to the brim inside the closets capacity.

Flick eyed the bags. "What's all that doing here?"

"All? Oh, no this is only half. The other half is at your warehouse. You know, the one you have my father being held hostage in."

The front door of the apartment exploded and before Flick could rebuttal there were several U.S. Marshal's swarming the room and putting her and her guard in cuffs. "You crazy son of a bitch what the hell is this!" Flick screamed at Jared.

Jared pointed to the bags of pills resting at his feet. "This is what you taught me Flick. It's just a few million in Lace, hiding in plain sight."

U.S. Marshal Marvin Price walked through the front door once Flick was secured. His first stop was the bathroom with a forensic specialist. After a moment he appeared in the bedroom and nodded in Jared's direction. On cue he reached down and removed the tape from Hailey's mouth and started to undo her restraints.

Price turned to Flick as she struggled to get at Jared. After realizing her efforts were futile, she shook her head in disgust as Jared pulled the wire out from under his shirt. "Guess we finally have something to tie you to, huh sweetheart?"

"Go to hell Price," Flick said. "I was here taking this junkie down and my lawyers are going to hand you your ass for this. Now let me go!"

"Not likely," Jared said. "Oh and Price? You might want to check her phone. She's mentioned something about keeping a tracking device on the whereabouts of the other half of her drug supply. Some kind of app or something."

"I've never seen that phone in my life you little shit," Flick said.

"No? Me either. But I'm sure it'll have your prints all over it." Jared had deleted the phones contents with the exception of the locator app. He had wiped it down and kept it in a cloth in his pocket. He knew that if he threw it in Flick's direction she'd catch it. Now it would serve as a link between the apartment and the warehouse; her prints would be the only one's on it.

He'd also placed a tile locator at the production house when he had gone to clean out the massive stockpile of Lace to place it all in each of the two locations. He left a few bags on the counters, of course, to tie her to that location as well. He'd also printed out contact sheet of every doctor, pharmacist and law enforcement individual Jared knew of that she had under her thumb and within her ring.

She spit in his direction and dug her red heels into the floor as they dragged her away. Price sauntered over to Jared's side, the two of them watching her carry on and curse.

"Can I ask you something?" Pierce asked, smiling in Flick's direction.

"Anything," Jared replied.

"When we first started listening in you said you had to give her something. What was it?"

Jared shrugged. "Oh…just the middle finger."

"Sure it wasn't a phone?"

"It was definitely not a phone."

Price nodded, his wide-toothed grin showing that he was complicit. "Of course not. Just had to check." He motioned toward the women as they had the last of their restraints removed and were being looked over by paramedics. "Don't be fooled by the turmoil in your gut wondering if you did the right thing here kid. You did. Your town won't ever be the same."

Jared opened his arms and Hailey slid into them, burying her face into his chest. His mom was shortly at his side, her arms struggling to encompass both of them and bring them close.

A warm smile spread across Jared's face as he let Price's words sink in. "Yeah," he murmured, enveloped in tranquility. "My town..."

ABOUT THE AUTHOR

K.L. Randis, author of bestselling novel *Spilled Milk* and the *Pillbillies* series, started journaling at the age of six and had short stories and poetry published by the time she was thirteen.

She is a graduate of Pennsylvania State University and a certified expert in the field of domestic violence. She has since written numerous local publications that brought awareness to domestic violence and child abuse. K.L. Randis engages audiences on a local and national level to raise awareness about child abuse, serving as a frequent commentator to media outlets. She has developed local high school presentations on teen dating violence and was named Community Woman of Distinction for 2011 by East Stroudsburg University.

Spilled Milk is her first novel, which grabbed the #1 bestsellers spot in the genre of *Child Abuse* on Amazon for eight consecutive months only 24 hours after it's debut. She resides in the Pocono Mountains of Pennsylvania.

Contact the Author:
www.klrandis.com
authorklrandis@gmail.com
Facebook: www.facebook.com/klrandis
Twitter: @KLRandis

Made in United States
North Haven, CT
24 January 2024